STONE ARCH BOOKS
a capstone imprint

Published by Stone Arch Books in 2016
A Capstone Imprint
1710 Roe Crest Drive
North Mankato, Minnesota 56003
www.mycapstone.com

STAR34870

Cataloging-in-Publication Data is available
at the Library of Congress website.
ISBN: 978-1-4965-2537-6 (library binding)
ISBN: 978-1-4965-2541-3 (paperback)
ISBN: 978-1-4965-2545-1 (eBook PDF)

Summary: Fun turns into fear when the Scarecrow takes
over the corn maze at the Gotham City Harvest Festival.
Now Batman and Robin race to rescue a group of
teens — including the governor's daughter — from the
nightmare maze. Can the Dynamic Duo capture
the Scarecrow in the twisting labyrinth despite their
worst fears?

Editor: Christopher Harbo
Designer: Hilary Wacholz

Printed in the United States of America in
North Mankato, Minnesota.
022016   009492R

BATMAN & ROBIN
ADVENTURES

SCARECROW'S
NIGHTMARE MAZE

BY J. E. BRIGHT

ILLUSTRATED BY
LUCIANO VECCHIO

BATMAN CREATED BY BOB KANE

TABLE OF CONTENTS

CHAPTER 1

SWITCHEROO

On a foggy autumn evening, Batman and Robin arrived at Arkham Asylum for a routine check. So many of their archenemies were imprisoned in the cells for the criminally insane that they visited regularly for inspection.

Dr. Jeremiah Arkham met them on a rooftop parapet. "It's been quiet," reported Dr. Arkham. Wisps of fog swirled around his legs as he led them down a stone spiral staircase into the shadowy asylum below.

"I don't like quiet," said Batman. "It means somebody's up to something." He wrinkled his nose behind his cowl. A scent smelled familiar.

Batman felt uneasy, as though some deep-seated fear was awakening inside him. He scowled at Dr. Arkham's back, wondering why his instincts were on high alert. There was a protective filter in the nose holes of his mask. His Batcomputer had analyzed the chemistry of the air and relayed its findings. Nothing seemed unusual, but his nerves were still on edge.

"Arkham's inmates are always plotting escape and revenge," said Robin.

"Mostly revenge against you two," replied Dr. Arkham. "But not only." He held open a metal door into the hall of holding cells and motioned for the Dynamic Duo to enter.

"Meaning what?" Robin asked, following Batman inside.

"So many of our patients are lost in their own deep-rooted obsessions," said Dr. Arkham. "Sometimes their psychoses target Batman because he imprisoned them. Other times, the symbolism of your fight against evil triggers their need for attention. But often these souls were lost long before they were ever introduced to the Dynamic Duo."

"They're here to be helped," replied Batman.

Dr. Arkham chuckled. "These criminals receive the most effective treatments known to modern psychiatry and biochemistry," he said. "But you know as well as I do, Batman, that many are held here because nowhere else can handle their dangerous madness."

The trio fell silent as they passed Poison Ivy's holding cell. Inside, she sat motionless on a plastic chair in the middle of a climate-controlled plastic box. Not a stray microbe or spore could be allowed inside.

Down the hall were the separate steel cells of Two-Face and Victor Zsasz. Both were locked behind solid vault doors. Nearby were the specialized holding tanks for Killer Croc, Clayface, and Bane. Killer Croc hissed in hatred as Batman, Robin, and the asylum's administrator walked by his swampy enclosure.

Bane was held inside a thick metal cylinder with no doors. All his vital signs were constantly monitored as the criminal superhuman recovered from addiction to the Venom that made him so dangerously powerful. Batman checked Bane's monitors.

"He's been calm," said Dr. Arkham.

"Let me know the second anything changes," replied Batman. Bane had hurt him too badly in the past for the villain ever to be allowed freedom again.

Dr. Arkham led Batman and Robin to the dark, barred compartment where Dr. Jonathan Crane, also known as the Scarecrow, now festered away his days. A hazy full moon shone down a beam through a high window. It illuminated Dr. Crane lying flat on his back on his cell floor. He wore a crude woven mask with slits for eyes and jagged sewn teeth.

"*Jack and Jill,*" mumbled the Scarecrow, "*went up a hill.*"

"How did he get his mask?" asked the Dark Knight. "He shouldn't have that. I'm afraid that's harmful to his mental state."

"We take them away regularly," replied Dr. Arkham. "But he always seems to find a way to make another. Once he wove one out of his own hair."

"Batman," said Robin. "You told me to warn you if you used any red flag words, like *scared* or *afraid*. Especially around the Scarecrow."

Batman narrowed his eyes. "He's always messing with our minds, playing with our fears. I don't like that I can't trust my own perceptions around him."

The Dark Knight shifted to look over the whole hallway. Wisps of fog swirled along the stone halls of the asylum. His Batcomputer readouts still showed no unusual chemicals in the air, but Batman knew computer data wasn't always the whole story.

"Something's wrong here," Batman said. "I can smell it."

"Is he gassing us?" asked Robin. The Scarecrow was known to use toxic fear gas to control people for his own insane research.

"I did say the word *afraid*," said Batman. "It's possible he's created a chemical formula we've never seen before, something my scans can't pick up. Stay alert."

"*Jack fell down*," said Dr. Arkham, blinking rapidly at Batman through his glasses, "*and broke his crown.*"

Batman and Robin took a step backward in alarm as Dr. Arkham grinned insanely at them. Then his teeth appeared to stretch until they resembled a sewn-up scar.

"That's not right," said Robin.

"My heart rate is rising," said Batman. "I'm sweating. I'm having the urge to flee or attack. These are symptoms of fear. We've been gassed. Don't trust your senses, Robin."

AAAHH! Dr. Arkham screamed. His face twisted and pulled like a warped reflection in a funhouse mirror. Batman's gut churned at the evil shapes of the doctor's face, but he stood firm, fighting the panic drying out his mouth. The doctor leaned forward, groaning and moaning as his whole body twisted and grew longer.

Then he stood up straight, much taller and skinnier. His churning face snapped into focus, now textured and ragged, covered by rough burlap. It was no longer Dr. Arkham. Instead, the Scarecrow stood in front of Batman and Robin. His wild eyes beamed down at them from inside his mask.

"And Jill came tumbling after," said the Scarecrow.

"He was the Scarecrow the whole time!" gasped Robin.

"We've imprisoned the wrong person," growled Batman. He felt dizzy with worry. There was little he dreaded more than locking the wrong person in jail. "Grab him before he gets away."

Batman and Robin shifted to flank the lanky villain. The Scarecrow backpedaled with his hands up before tilting to the side and swinging his gawky leg at Robin.

Robin slid under the Scarecrow's heel, striking his own boot into the villain's other ankle. **BAM!** The Scarecrow hopped in pain, then he swiveled around to throw a punch at Batman.

With an effortless sidestep, Batman avoided the Scarecrow's fist. Batman chopped out with his forearm and the Scarecrow twisted around his attack. The villain slid to the side to strike with his creepy long fingernails.

His cape swirling to mask his movements, Batman turned away from the villain's slicing fingernails. He quickly spun back toward the Scarecrow. Then he grabbed the middle of the Scarecrow's long arm and yanked it, pulling the villain off-balance. The Scarecrow sprawled forward onto his face on the floor. Batman dropped his knee on the Scarecrow's bony back, pinning him down securely.

"Open Dr. Crane's cell!" Batman said to a redheaded orderly in her glass office. Her eyes were wide with fear.

Frantically, the orderly pressed a button, and a door of iron bars slid open. **CLANG!**

"Check if that's Jeremiah Arkham in the cell," Batman said to Robin.

Robin ran inside and pulled the Scarecrow mask off the person lying down. It was Dr. Arkham!

AAAHH! Dr. Arkham screamed at the sight of Robin. "The face of madness!" he shrieked. "We're all mad here!" Then he went still, his eyes staring blankly.

Robin dragged Dr. Arkham out of the cell, and Batman shoved the Scarecrow inside.

"I don't know how he got out," said Batman, "but he must have drugged us the moment we arrived."

"You mean he made us believe he was Dr. Arkham?" Robin asked.

"Yes," Batman replied. "He's playing on our fears. At least the villain is inside and the administrator is safe now. The Scarecrow's not getting out of this cell past me."

Holding up the Scarecrow mask, Robin grimaced. "I hope this isn't the one made out of his hair." He dropped it beside the doctor on the floor.

Batman stepped out into the corridor. "Lock him in," he told the orderly. "Now!"

The female guard jammed her finger down on a button, and the cell's iron bars rolled shut. **CLANK!**

"I wonder how he got out in the first place," said Batman. His breathing was better, and he didn't feel so afraid. A weight had lifted from his chest. He suddenly felt foolish that he'd been scared of imprisoning the wrong person.

"I feel much better with the real villain behind bars," said Robin.

"Funny," said Batman. "I was just thinking the opposite." He glanced down at Dr. Arkham on the floor behind him, but the administrator had vanished entirely. "Look."

Robin jumped. "He was right there!"

"The mask is gone, too," Batman noticed. They turned to face the cell.

The man inside sat up and pulled off his mask.

It was Dr. Arkham. He blinked behind his glasses, staring through the cell's bars at Batman and Robin. Dr. Arkham frowned, looking bewildered as to how he'd gotten locked inside.

"Are we still hallucinating?" asked Robin.

"My mind's a blur and my pulse is racing," mumbled Dr. Arkham. "What happened?"

"We've been tricked into setting the Scarecrow free," said Batman.

CHAPTER 2

ENTER THE NIGHTMARE

"We were manipulated with fear hallucinations," said Batman. "I hate when he does that. The Scarecrow played into my fear of imprisoning the wrong person, while using Dr. Arkham's fear of turning into one of his patients."

Batman turned to Dr. Arkham. "So he convinced us that you were the Scarecrow, and that you were the one we needed to lock up," he said. "In effect, you *became* him momentarily. The gas is becoming more subtle as he perfects it."

Robin tightened his gloves to fists. "He sure fooled me."

"I would say this is a new type of attack from our dear Dr. Crane," said Dr. Arkham. "We all saw the same false visions. Yes, I believed I was the Scarecrow, temporarily, and that was a horrible experience. I don't believe we've seen him create fear hallucinations that are shared by multiple people before."

"Shared delusions," said Robin. "That's just great."

"His madness is spreading," said Batman.

"Find him, please," said Dr. Arkham. "He's incredibly dangerous. He could scare innocent people . . . to death."

"I'll get him, Dr. Arkham," said Batman. "I'm scary, too."

He and Robin raced through Arkham Asylum, rushing up to the Batcopter they had left on the roof.

"We'll search the city from the air," said Batman as he strapped himself into the pilot's seat.

WHOOSH! The Batcopter rose straight up. Batman swooped it through Gotham's skyline, staying low enough to inspect the streets, but high enough that the citizens didn't notice the silent aircraft.

"What are we looking for?" asked Robin.

"Mayhem," replied Batman. "And fear."

The police scanner squawked with incoming reports of a robbery near the theater district on the south side of the city. The cops barked their calls for backup in confused and terrified voices.

"The sounds of the Scarecrow," said Batman grimly. He steered the Batcopter toward the disturbance.

Batman and Robin flew over a small, nervous crowd gathered outside a storehouse with a retail front at street level. Two police cars blocked the onlookers from getting too close. An open ambulance idled nearby, its colorful lights flashing in the night. Quickly, Batman landed the copter on the roof, and he and Robin scrambled down the fire escape in an alley. They rushed up to Detective Bullock standing beside a squad car.

"Batman," said Bullock, shaking his head, "look at this mess."

"Where's the Scarecrow?" asked Batman.

"Gone," Bullock replied. "It was only a minor robbery, but that creep gassed all the employees inside."

"What kind of effect did the gas have on them?" Batman asked.

"They thought they were being attacked by ravens," Bullock said.

Robin shuddered in sympathy. "What kind of business do they work for? What was stolen?"

"It's a prop warehouse," answered Detective Bullock. "You know for movies, plays, and TV shows? They rent out all kinds of things. We're still trying to find out what was taken, but it doesn't appear to be anything of great value."

"Are the employees still here?" Batman asked.

"In the ambulance," said Bullock. "Go easy on them — they're traumatized. They've had the fright of their lives."

Batman and Robin peeked into the back of the ambulance, where two emergency workers helped a man and a woman on stretchers. Another man sat up on a side bench with a cloth covering his face.

"We need to ask you a few questions," Batman told the man on the bench. "Who is the manager of the prop warehouse?"

The man lowered his cloth. He had scratches on his face, but was otherwise unhurt. "I am," he said. "Ask away, Batman. Hello, Robin. I want to help you guys capture that maniac."

"What did the Scarecrow steal?" asked Robin.

The manager let out a painful snort of laughter. "Only two things are missing," he replied. "A classic black-tie tuxedo and . . . an old farming tool. A scythe."

Robin winced. "The long pole with the wicked curved blade on the end?"

"That's the thing," said the manager. "It was used for cutting grain, but it makes a nasty weapon. It's not a fake blade, either. It's seriously sharp."

"Thank you for the information," said Batman. "I hope you and your team make a full recovery."

"Just get that creep," said the manager. "That's the main thing."

"We'll get him," said Batman.

With Robin a step behind, Batman rushed back up to the roof and into the Batcopter.

"I have a good idea where the Scarecrow's going," said Batman, as he launched the copter upward. "What are the major events in Gotham City this weekend?"

Robin considered the question. "The high school students are all going to their Harvest Prom this weekend. Is that why he stole a fancy tuxedo?"

"Perhaps," said Batman. "Did you know the Scarecrow's first crime was after his own prom? He was mocked by the other students for his awkward dancing, and he got revenge. Something to keep in mind. But there's a bigger event . . . which the prom kids will attend, too."

"The Gotham City Harvest Festival is this weekend," said Robin. "The scythe makes more sense now."

"Right. A high school prom after-party at the Harvest Festival. He won't be able to resist," said Batman.

"Of course," said Robin.

Batman steered the Batcopter through the darkness out of the city. The festival actually took place past Gotham City's outskirts, near one of the last farms remaining in the area.

It was a weekend fair with bake-offs, rodeo shows, carnival rides, Halloween costume contests, and food tents. But its biggest attraction was the world-famous Gotham City corn maze. A field of corn was the natural habitat for any scarecrow with a scythe!

It didn't take long for Batman to fly the Batcopter to the fairgrounds, buzzing high above the busy festival lights below. He was certain that the Scarecrow would head straight to the fair. The villain would be drawn to the scope of the terror he could inflict on the fairgoers in a spooky Halloween-themed setting.

Batman and Robin hovered in the copter just above the line of hazy clouds, staying hidden from the people below. Through gaps in the clouds, Batman peered down at the glow of the main concert stage, the rows of illuminated booths, and the crowds around the food tents.

"I can practically smell the fried dough from up here," said Robin.

"Don't let your imagination run away with you," replied Batman. "That could be very dangerous when dealing with the Scarecrow." He tilted his head at the thousands of little reddish LED lights outlining complicated pathways on the edge of the fair. "That's the maze," he said. "It's ten acres of confusing corn. If I were the Scarecrow, that's where I would focus my attack. Let's find someplace to land."

Batman set the Batcopter down behind a large medical tent. He and Robin hurried through the shadowy alleys behind the booths, stepping over extension cords, avoiding the crowds as they made their way toward the corn maze.

"Be very aware of anything unusual," Batman warned Robin. "Any kind of strange vision could mean we're feeling the effects of the Scarecrow's gas."

"Expect the unexpected," said Robin. "Gotcha."

"Expect a nightmare," said Batman.

EEEEE!

As if on cue, a girl's scream pierced the sounds of the crowd. That first scream was followed by a chorus of more shrieks coming from the direction of the corn maze.

The atmosphere at the fair quickly became uneasy as the screams unnerved all the attendees. Between the booths, Batman could see the people in the throng stopping suddenly, bumping into one another, as the screams made them worried and nervous.

"We've got to put a stop to whatever's going on," said Batman, "or this crowd is going to panic. People will get trampled."

Batman and Robin slipped out from behind the booths at the edge of the cornfield. Robin had to backtrack suddenly when Batman stopped abruptly in front of a snack shack.

"One bag of peanuts," said Batman.

"Sure," the teenager working in the booth replied, handing him a sack of peanuts in their shells. "No charge for you, Batman."

"What are those for?" asked Robin, as they continued along the edge of the corn.

"You'll see," Batman replied.

Outside the arched wooden entrance to the maze, groups of police officers huddled together under LED torches. More cops comforted civilians nearby, while others set up a perimeter with yellow tape, holding back random rubbernecking fairgoers.

"There's Commissioner Gordon," said Robin, "talking to Governor Stonefellow."

"Hmm," said Batman, as they hurried over, ducking under the tape. "The governor looks like he's seen a ghost."

"Batman!" Governor Stonefellow gasped, his eyes red and wild. "You have to save her!"

Batman glanced at Commissioner Gordon for clarification.

"His teenage daughter, Stacey," Gordon explained. "She's trapped inside the corn maze with that maniac the Scarecrow. We have no idea what's going on in there, but a bunch of high school students were caught in the maze when the Scarecrow took it over. They were celebrating after their Harvest Prom earlier this evening. Only those teenagers are inside with the Scarecrow. Everyone else managed to escape, which I doubt was an accident."

"I agree," said Batman. "The Scarecrow always has reasons, as insane as they are."

AAAIIEEEE!

A fresh shriek cut through the corn. It was a girl, sounding horrified. The deeper screams of young men and scared sobs of other girls joined her terror.

"What's he doing to them?" asked Governor Stonefellow. "Batman, you know I don't approve of your methods . . . but do whatever you can to get Stacey out of that nightmare!"

"I will," said Batman. "Ready, Robin?"

"I'm ready," said Robin.

"To get them out," said Batman, "we have to enter the nightmare ourselves."

The police officers moved aside to let Batman and Robin into the dark, misty murkiness of the corn maze.

CHAPTER 3

FEEL THE FEAR

As he and Robin walked cautiously into the eerie maze cut into the cornfield, Batman called up a GPS satellite image on the Batcomputer built into his cowl. He could see the maze, but the image from orbit wasn't sharp enough to see the pathways clearly in the murky night. The satellite feed just looked like a complicated field of tiny red LED lights strung irregularly along the trails through the corn.

"Can you see the best path to follow?" Robin asked.

"No, the movement of the tall stalks causes the red lights to flicker from above," Batman replied. "Let's keep taking right turns and generally head toward the screams."

"I don't hear anything now," said Robin. "The corn absorbs sound. There's only its rustling as it sways in the wind. It's freaky."

Batman turned a corner in the maze and grimaced as he saw deeper puddles of fog floating between the cornrows. "I wish I'd developed a better filter for the Scarecrow's fear gas," he said. "The base chemical triggers a fight-or-flight response in humans, but Dr. Crane has tinkered with the formula, creating his own mysterious toxin. He's an evil genius at chemistry, so the filter only buys us a few moments of clarity."

"I'm keeping my gas mask on," said Robin. "Even if it only slows down the effects, that might give us some tiny advantage."

"We'll need every edge we can manage," agreed Batman.

They wandered down another aisle through the dense cornstalks. The red LED lights made the corn look sinister as its dry, wide leaves wavered in the breeze.

Batman stopped when they reached a three-way intersection. "From here it's all left turns back to the entrance of the maze," said Batman. He placed a peanut on the ground to mark the path back. "Take some peanuts and mark your direction when necessary."

Robin dumped two handfuls of peanuts into a pouch on his Utility Belt. "I hope I don't get hungry."

"We should split up," said Batman. "Because of the Scarecrow's history, we have a good idea why he is tormenting these teenagers. He always works toward his insane reasons, and that information may be our only hope of defeating him. Remember that he returns to situations that frighten him. He studies fear to try to regain control. That's also why he uses fear as a weapon."

"Don't you use fear, too?" asked Robin.

"I do," replied Batman. "The difference is that the Scarecrow gets excited by the terror of innocent people. It fascinates and thrills him. I use fear to strike at the cowardly heart of the guilty."

Robin nodded. "That's a big difference."

Batman glowered into the darkness. "Indeed," he said.

The Dark Knight studied the pathways in all three directions as far as he could see. "Take the left fork. Judging by the footprints, girls have walked that way in high-heeled shoes recently. See how those footprints are spaced far apart? Some of them were running. I'll follow the big boot prints to the right."

"Got it," said Robin. "We'll stop the Scarecrow's crazy vendetta." He headed toward the center path.

"Don't trust your senses," Batman warned. "Your fear may be fake but take action when you're really in danger."

Robin stopped and looked back. "How am I supposed to know?"

"You won't," replied Batman. "That's why the Scarecrow has always been one of our most dangerous enemies."

With a nod, Robin continued to stride down the center path. After the first turn away from Batman, the trail through the stalks zigged and zagged.

Soon Robin felt turned around. His compass told him which way was north, but it didn't feel right. A heavy silence fell across the dark field, punctuated only by the faint chirp of distant crickets. Even though Robin could walk as stealthily as a ninja, his lightest footstep still seemed to echo in the creepy quiet.

The next turn was only a two-way, so Robin took the path on the right. It curved slowly for a long stretch and entered into a lengthy straightaway. Overhead, a gibbous moon glowed orange behind a hazy layer of wafting clouds. He could see no stars in the overcast sky.

As he walked, Robin recalled the training Batman had given him about fear. He needed to let himself feel it. Ignoring or denying fear would only blindside him later. The important thing was to recognize when he was afraid, but not give in to it. "Bravery is taking honorable action in the face of fear," Robin reminded himself in a whisper.

He reached a four-way intersection and marked the way he had come with a peanut. He took the rightmost path and continued on through a series of short, choppy turns.

Deep into the maze now, Robin sharpened all of his senses, on high alert. He smelled the sweet, drying corn and the rich soil. The air had the first chill of autumn. The sounds of the festival seemed very far away, and even the crickets had fallen silent.

Robin closed his eyes to focus on his sense of hearing. Out of the silence, the softest of sounds reached his ears. He heard the murmur of young voices whispering.

Creeping quietly along the trail, Robin fell in behind a teenage boy and girl who were tiptoeing down a connecting path. He followed them for a few feet. The young man was medium height and almost as muscular as Robin himself. He was dressed in a rental tuxedo and held a rake in his hand as a weapon. The young woman wore a silvery gown, and her high-heeled shoes dangled from the straps in one hand.

"Shh," said Robin.

The couple whirled around. The boy held up the rake, and the girl hurled her shoes at Robin. *SWISH!*

The shoes whizzed past Robin's head as he sidestepped. "It's okay," he whispered. "Don't be frightened."

"Look, it's the Boy Wonder," the girl said, nudging the teen boy. "Robin, are you here to rescue us?"

"I am," replied Robin. He raised his finger to his lips. "But, really, shh. Are you both okay? Have either of you been hurt?"

"We're fine," the girl said softly. "I'm Stacey Stonefellow. Is Batman somewhere in the maze, too?"

"He is," said Robin. "He's going after the Scarecrow. The governor — I mean your father — is really worried about you. All of you. Do you know if anyone in your group has been harmed?"

"I don't think so," Stacey said. "Not physically. We were just terrified out of our minds."

She grabbed onto the guy's arm and pulled him toward Robin. He lowered his rake as he drew near.

"This is my boyfriend, Carlos," Stacey said. "We just won queen and king of the Gotham City Harvest Dance tonight. Now look at us, sneaking away from some maniac in a corn maze. And I just threw my expensive shoes at you. Sorry about that."

"No worries," said Robin. He glanced at the familiar way Carlos was holding his rake. "Lacrosse?"

"Captain of the varsity team," Carlos replied with a smile.

"How are you going to stop that nut case?" asked Stacey. "He's totally freaking out my friends. Something really terrible is going on, and I'm sick of feeling afraid. I want out of this horrible maze now, but we keep getting lost. Now that you're here, we can fight back, right? So what are we going to do?"

"I'm hatching a plan," said Robin. "It's risky, and dangerous, but I could use your help if you're up for it.

"We're in," said Carlos.

Stacey narrowed her eyes. "Totally."

CHAPTER 4

MAN ON FIRE

After following what seemed like endless paths and switchbacks, and marking a half-dozen intersections with peanuts, Batman heard something that stopped him cold. Soft footsteps, and low sobbing, filtered through the border of corn rows to his right.

As quietly as he could, the Dark Knight stepped into the wide corn border. The stalks were planted so close together that he had to pry them apart. One row at a time, he pushed through the divider.

SSSHHH! SSSHHH! The corn's sharp leaves with their serrated edges tugged at his Batsuit and cape. He might have gotten multiple fine cuts if he wasn't protected by the strongest fabric alloys money could buy.

When he reached the other side of the wall, Batman hid in the darkness a few stalks back. He peered through the corn.

The Scarecrow circled around a wide clearing in the maze, holding an enormous scythe in his bony hands. He was wearing a snazzy tuxedo that was a few sizes too small, and his wrists stuck out of the jacket. The pants were several inches too short, too, showing his long, thin ankles.

A group of seven or eight teenagers huddled together in the middle, all wearing formal dress. The teens sobbed and clung to each other in terror.

"I don't want to get burned," one girl moaned.

A young man hugged her tighter. "Please let us out of here," he begged the Scarecrow.

The Scarecrow grinned wide, enjoying their fright. He swung the scythe's wicked blade above the teenagers' heads. *SWOOSH!* He chuckled as they ducked lower and let out desperate cries.

Billows of greenish gas puffed out of the Scarecrow's too-short sleeves. *HISSS!* Whatever the gas made the teens see, it was truly horrific.

Then the gas passed through Batman's mask filter. When it reached his nose, the entire clearing ignited in a fiery inferno before his eyes.

FWOOSH!

He didn't know if the fire had just started, or if he had suddenly begun seeing the same thing the teens were experiencing. All he knew was that his heart pounded as the terrible heat of the fire scalded his eyes.

Dancing awkwardly around the teenagers, still howling with laughter, the Scarecrow blazed with flames. His scythe swooped through the burning air, trailing tongues of fire that spread to the dry corn on all sides.

Like any sane person threatened by raging fire, Batman felt deeply afraid for his life.

* * *

"Tell me exactly what you saw," Robin said to Stacey and Carlos.

"You tell him," Stacey instructed Carlos. "I'm exhausted."

"The Scarecrow," explained Carlos, "came out of nowhere. He blocked us into a corner of the maze, in this wider open area. Stacey and I, we were on the edge, so when I saw his crazy mask and smoke coming out of his tuxedo sleeves, I pulled her into the corn." He raised his hand to show Robin raw scratches from the cornstalk leaves. "We got out of range and stayed quiet to watch."

"It was so scary," Stacey added. "We were hidden, but our friends were totally exposed to the gas. I could see their faces when it hit them." She shuddered. "I have never seen anyone look so scared in my life. My friend Annie was screaming like she was spinning out in a car accident."

"My friend Dominic is a tough dude," said Carlos, "but even he was yelling."

"Did the Scarecrow say anything?" asked Robin. "Anything you remember?"

Carlos rubbed his eyebrow with the back of his hand. "He was singing something," he said. "What do you call it?"

"A nursery rhyme," Stacey filled in. "That one that goes, '*Georgie Porgie, pudding and pie, kissed the girls and made them cry.*' It was totally creepy."

"Hmm," said Robin. "Anything else?"

"Yeah," replied Carlos. "Something horrible. Like, 'Your screams are music I can really dance to. Not making fun of me now, are you?'"

"And then he said, 'Payback hurts, doesn't it,'" said Stacey. "Then, uh, 'I drink your fear like delicious party punch,' I think. Something bonkers like that."

"You two have been very helpful," said Robin, "but if you can be brave, I've got one more task for you. It could be a lot more dangerous, and you'll have to get the other kids to follow your lead —"

"They do that anyway," said Stacey with a sniff. "That's how we became queen and king."

"It's cool if you don't want to put yourself in danger," said Robin. "You'll have to face some very scary fears."

"The Scarecrow needs to be taken down," said Stacey. She grabbed Carlos' hand, and he nodded. "Bring it on."

"One more thing," said Robin. He nodded toward Carlos' rake. "Do you mind if I borrow that stick?"

* * *

From his hiding place in the corn on the edge of the clearing, Batman watched the inferno blaze ever closer. Fear gas seeped between the bases of the cornstalks, twining around Batman's boots.

Panic fluttered in Batman's chest. He wanted to take deep breaths to calm himself, but that would only bring more of the gas into his lungs.

Batman hugged himself tightly as the Scarecrow laughed and danced around the cowering teens.

"Georgie Porgie, pudding and pie," the Scarecrow sang, his limbs jerking in an awful dance. **SHOOSH!** He swept his burning scythe over the shrieking teenagers' heads as fire surrounded him in flickering flames. *"Kissed the girls and made them cry."*

Batman had never been more frightened. It was so difficult to remember that the fear was caused by the gas. Watching the fire and the madman in the middle of it swirling his scythe, Batman broke out in a hot sweat. He wanted to curl up in a ball and give up. He had the urge to run and never look back.

The teens screamed again, and Batman tightened his hands to fists. It didn't matter that he was scared. There was a real enemy to face with all the bravery he could summon. Innocent kids were in danger. This was no time to fall prey to his own fears. He could help. The teens needed him.

Batman pulled a canister off his Utility Belt. He launched himself out of the corn, barreling full-speed toward the Scarecrow. *"When the boys came out to play,"* yelled Batman, *"Georgie Porgie ran away!"*

The Scarecrow reeled away in surprise, trying to get his scythe up to slice Batman.

Batman ducked under the swinging blade and pressed a button on the canister. **_FSSSHHH!_**

A thick spray of foam spewed out. It coated the Scarecrow from mask to boots, extinguishing his fire.

The Scarecrow bellowed in fury, scrambling at the foam, wiping it off his mask and arms.

"Come on," Batman growled at the group of teenagers. "Follow me!"

As Batman herded the formally-dressed teens down a path, the Scarecrow managed to scrape the foam off himself. New clouds of fear gas issued from his shirt and pant cuffs, roiling toward Batman.

"Faster," urged Batman, pushing the kids to run down the path.

The Scarecrow followed in a rush, swinging his scythe, flames once again surrounding him.

FWOOSH!

The corn ignited on either side of him, exploding with fire.

The fire probably was just a hallucination, Batman knew, but he couldn't take that chance. The Scarecrow was horrible enough to really use fire and boost it with delusions that made it seem worse, with real danger at the core.

"Batman!" a girl yelled from the front of the group. "We're trapped."

Batman glanced over the teenagers. They had hit a dead end.

The Scarecrow slowed down, knowing he had them cornered. He milked the frightening moment.

SWOOSH!

He sliced his scythe in front of him, fire raging all around him in scorching sprays of flame.

The group of teens pressed against the back wall of corn, with Batman shielding them with his cape outstretched. "Stop this, Scarecrow!" Batman said. "These kids have done nothing to you!"

"They're all the same," said the Scarecrow, his eyes shining behind his mask in whirling balls of fire. "They would laugh if I didn't make them scream. How delightful that I can make them so frightened, so terrified of me, that they will never find joy in laughter again in their lives!"

The Scarecrow raised his hand, and an army of bats fluttered down into the maze, flapping and squeaking overhead. *EEK! EEK! EEK!*

"I'm not afraid of bats," said Batman.

"But they are," replied the Scarecrow. "Now they will feel what I feel, and you will feel what they feel!" *FSSST!* Fogs of gas gusted out of his jacket collar. It billowed out from under his mask.

Now Batman fully felt terror. The Scarecrow's new fear gas formula connected him to the teens' phobia. He felt their terrible panic over the frightening flapping of the bats. For the first time, he understood his effect on the cowardly criminals he intimidated with his own image, and he was afraid.

Batman also sensed what the teenagers were experiencing, and their fear echoed inside him in a connected circuit of horror. Again he wanted to run, to escape into the corn, but he couldn't allow himself to abandon the helpless innocent teenagers.

"Scarecrow!" Robin yelled as he jumped out of a border of corn behind the villain. "Your reign of terror ends now!" Robin raised the wooden handle of a farm tool, spinning it in front of him like a bo staff, his weapon of choice.

"No, Robin!" yelled Batman, lost in his dread. "Run!"

CHAPTER 5

CONFUSE HIM WITH KINDNESS

With a shriek of rage, the Scarecrow charged at Robin. As he ran, he flapped his skinny arms at the Boy Wonder, swinging his fiery scythe in terrifying arcs. Fire continued to blaze all around him.

SHIING! Robin parried the scythe with his staff. But the fury of the Scarecrow's attack forced him to back up. Robin quickly regained his balance and readied his stance to go on the offensive.

Batman bit his lip worriedly as Robin lunged forward, sweeping his staff at the Scarecrow's legs.

The Scarecrow jumped over the staff and swung downward with his scythe, missing Robin's head by centimeters.

Stepping forward, Batman followed the fight as his partner flipped and rolled backward. Robin jumped back up in ready position, swirling his staff over his head.

The Scarecrow laughed maniacally, his gawky body jittering as he tried to slice Robin with his burning blade.

Robin ducked, bringing his bo staff up to block the scythe. But when the staff and scythe collided, the staff burst into flame. **FOOM!** Robin was forced to drop the burning wooden weapon.

BAM! The Scarecrow bashed Robin in the chest with the top of the scythe. It didn't cut Robin, but knocked him over, toppling him onto his back.

"No!" screamed Batman. This was his absolute worst fear: that the people who he had sworn to protect might be hurt while helping him fight.

The Scarecrow, chuckling darkly, advanced on Robin. Batman's head swam as he fought the fury and fear flooding his system. The Scarecrow seemed so much larger than life, like a terrorizing monster.

Batman had to remember that all these frightening emotions were not his own. But how could he stand up against such a horrifying supernatural creature dealing fire and destruction? He was only an ordinary man, fighting a beast from the underworld.

One of the Scarecrow's bats fluttered into Batman's face, and he flicked it away with the back of his hand.

But his hand swept right through it. The bats were only visions. They weren't real.

"I've got to clear away some of this gas," muttered Batman. "It's my only chance."

He raised a transmitter from his Utility Belt and pressed a button. A subsonic signal echoed out into the night.

Maybe hallucination bats could be battled with real bats. Lots of real bats.

A second later, hundreds and hundreds of little brown bats responded to Batman's call, fluttering above the corn maze. *EEK! EEK! EEK!* They flapped their leathery wings, blowing away the gas.

Batman pulled himself to his feet. As the air cleared, so did his mind.

The Scarecrow was only a man, too. His name was Dr. Jonathan Crane. He had no superpowers. Just like Batman. Everything else was just an awful illusion.

Hurtling himself forward, Batman whacked the Scarecrow in the back. **SMACK!**

The criminal stumbled, and Robin scrambled out of the way. Then the Scarecrow wheeled around with surprising dexterity, hacking at Batman with his scythe.

Batman sidestepped, and he kicked the Scarecrow again. He swirled his cape as he jumped behind the Scarecrow, striking the villain's right arm. **WHACK!**

Screaming in frustration, the Scarecrow chopped at Batman, but couldn't catch him.

SWOOSH! Batman bowed low under another swing of the scythe and then knocked the Scarecrow over.

The Scarecrow plopped backward, howling in fury.

"Now!" yelled Robin.

Carlos and Stacey stepped around the corner. They smiled at the Scarecrow with big, friendly expressions.

"Jonathan," said Stacey. "You should totally dance with us."

"We're all having fun," said Carlos. "Don't be the odd man out. We want you to join us and have a good time."

While the Scarecrow gaped at the teenagers in shocked surprise, Stacey motioned with her hand for her friend Annie to step forward.

Annie gulped, but she stood bravely next to Stacey and smiled warmly at the Scarecrow. "Yeah," she said, "we should be having a blast, not stuck in this dreary corn maze. You're too cute to be so angry, Jonathan."

Carlos reached down and helped his friend Dominic up to his feet.

"Come on, dude," said Dominic. "Don't be a downer. We could be having the best time."

"Join the party," added Robin. "Everyone is welcome. You just have to take your place."

The Scarecrow blinked at the teenagers, his eyes whirling behind his mask. "You're trying to trick me!" he screamed. "My peers were never interested in my friendship! They only wanted to hurt me . . . but I hurt them first!"

"That was then," said Stacey. "This is now. We're all much more accepting now."

"We know that there are all kinds of cool," said a brainy-looking kid with a bad haircut. His girlfriend nodded and hugged him.

"Jonathan," said Carlos. "Don't leave us hanging."

"You liars!" the Scarecrow said. "You mocked me and you will pay! I'll destroy you all just like I did back at my own prom!" He leaped up and tried to grab Carlos.

Robin jumped between them, bashing the Scarecrow back with his charred staff. **BAM!** "Jonathan, my friend," said Robin, "don't be like that."

Screaming in frustration, the Scarecrow flailed his gawky limbs and ran off into the corn maze.

"I'll get him," said Batman, and he sprinted after the Scarecrow.

The Scarecrow was fast on his long legs. Batman had to run full speed to avoid losing him in the maze. It would be so easy to get lost now, barreling though the dark corridors of corn. Through one turn after another, Batman managed to see a glimpse of which way the Scarecrow chose to run. But if he didn't find a way to catch up, the Scarecrow would vanish into the maze and regroup. Batman had to find him now, while the villain was still emotionally off-balance.

Then the Scarecrow scurried down the right fork in a three-way intersection.

Batman spotted a peanut on the ground, marking the center path. He didn't know if it was his or Robin's. But he knew it was the more direct way out.

Using his last reserves of speed, Batman charged down the center aisle, racing through a long diagonal alley. He came out at another intersection, seconds ahead of the Scarecrow.

Batman surprised the Scarecrow and landed a solid punch in the middle of his mask. **CRACK!** Then he kicked the Scarecrow precisely on the side of his head, knocking the villain unconscious.

"The Scarecrow is in my custody," he said to Robin over his two-way radio. "Make for the exit."

Then he dragged the Scarecrow out of the maze and released him to the waiting police.

"Everyone is safe," Batman informed the worried parents. A few moments later, Robin and the teenagers sprinted out of the maze. The teens all got big hugs from their families.

After Batman and Robin were congratulated by Commissioner Gordon, Governor Stonefellow and Stacey came over to shake their hands. The other teenagers gathered around the Dynamic Duo, too.

"You guys were awesome," said Stacey.

"Couldn't have done it without you," Robin replied with a grin.

"Okay, this was the scariest night," said Carlos, "but the most exciting, too."

"Exciting?" cried Annie. "I thought we were going to get burned alive or eaten by bats."

"And instead you were saved by them," said Batman. "Funny how our fears are often the things that keep us safe."

"I am deeply grateful," said Governor Stonefellow. He gave Stacey a tight hug.

"Let's go," said Batman. He and Robin vanished into the shadows, hurrying toward the Batcopter.

"Good work in there tonight," said Robin as they climbed in. "Neither of us gave in to our fears, and now Jonathan Crane will be back behind bars where he belongs."

"Still, I'm not happy," said Batman. "It was my fault the Scarecrow escaped Arkham Asylum in the first place. I hate being manipulated by his fear gas. We must find a way to neutralize it, to find filters that work with his newest formulas. Until we do that, the Scarecrow will always be a threat to Gotham City."

"We'll work on it," said Robin. "But now, let's just go home. I don't know about you, but I've been craving peanuts and popcorn for hours."

SCARECROW

REAL NAME: **Professor Jonathan Crane**

OCCUPATION: **Professional Criminal**

BASE: **Gotham City**

HEIGHT: **6 feet**

WEIGHT: **140 pounds**

HAIR: **Brown**

Jonathan Crane's obsession with fear took hold at an early age. Terrorized by bullies, Crane sought to free himself of his own worst fears. As he researched the subject of dread, Crane developed a strong understanding of fear. Using this knowledge, Crane overcame his tormentors by using their worst fears against them. This victory led to his transformation into the creepy super-villain, the Scarecrow.

- Crane became a professor at Gotham University to further his terrifying research. But when his colleagues took notice of his twisted experiments, they had him fired. To get revenge, Crane became the Scarecrow to try to frighten his enemies to death.

- Crane doesn't use conventional weaponry. Instead, he invented a Fear Toxin that causes his victims to hallucinate, bringing their worst fears and phobias to life. The gas makes the weak and gangly Crane look like a fearsome predator in the eyes of his prey.

- Crane's mastery of fear has come in handy. While locked up in Arkham Asylum, Crane once escaped by scaring two guards into releasing him!

BIOGRAPHIES

J. E. Bright is the author of many novels, novelizations, and novelty books for children and young adults. He lives in a sunny apartment in the Washington Heights neighborhood of Manhattan, with his difficult but soft female cat, Mabel, and his sweet male cat, Bernard. Find out more about J. E. Bright on his website.

Luciano Vecchio was born in 1982 and currently lives in Buenos Aires, Argentina. With experience in illustration, animation, and comics, his works have been published in the US, Spain, UK, France, and Argentina. His credits include *Ben 10* (DC Comics), *Cruel Thing* (Norma), *Unseen Tribe* (Zuda Comics), and *Sentinels* (Drumfish Productions).

GLOSSARY

contort (kuhn-TORT)—to twist into strange positions

delusion (di-LOO-zhuhn)—a false idea or a hallucination

hallucinate (huh-loo-suh-NAYT)—to hear or see things that are not really there

instinct (IN-stingkt)—behavior that is natural rather than learned

intimidate (in-TIM-uh-date)—to threaten in order to force certain behavior

manipulate (muh-NIP-yuh-late)—to change something in a clever way to influence people to do or think how you want

parapet (PA-ruh-paht)—a low wall or railing to protect the edge of a platform or roof

perception (pur-SEP-shuhn)—an understanding of the world through the senses of sight, smell, touch, taste, and hearing

perimeter (puh-RIM-uh-tur)—the outer edge or boundary of an area

psychiatry (sye-KYE-uh-tree)—the study and treatment of emotional and mental illness

scythe (SITHE)—a tool with a large curved blade used for cutting grass or crops by hand

DISCUSSION QUESTIONS

1. Why do you think the Scarecrow's past caused him to become a super-villain? Would he have turned out differently if he hadn't been bullied in school? Why or why not?

2. Why do Batman and Robin split up after they enter the corn maze? Should they have stayed together instead? Explain your answers.

3. Why did Robin need Stacey and Carlos' help? Could he and Batman have stopped the Scarecrow without their help? Discuss your answers.

WRITING PROMPTS

1. Batman and Robin use peanuts to mark their path through the corn maze. Write a short story set in a labyrinth or forest where your hero needs a method for finding his or her way out.

2. The Dynamic Duo passed the cells of several other super-villains in Arkham Asylum. Write a story where one of them escapes. Will Batman and Robin be able to capture this foe as well? You decide.

3. The Scarecrow tries to use Batman's fears against him, but the Dark Knight overcomes those fears. Write about a time you had to overcome your own fears, and explain how you did it.